Love,
Crazy Grandma
xo

G-REX

by Teri Daniels

illustrated by
Tracey Campbell Pearson

ORCHARD BOOKS
New York

Orchard Books, A Grolier Company
95 Madison Avenue, New York, NY 10016

Manufactured in the United States of America
Printed and bound by Phoenix Color Corp.
Book design by Kristina Albertson
The text of this book is set in 14 point Veljovic Book.
The illustrations are watercolor.
1 3 5 7 9 10 8 6 4 2

Library of Congress Cataloging-in-Publication Data
Daniels, Teri.
G-Rex / by Teri Daniels ; illustrations by Tracey Campbell Pearson.
p.   cm.
Summary: Six-year-old Gregory deals with his annoying older brother, Mark,
by turning into fierce G-Rex and threatening to eat him.
ISBN 0-531-30243-1 (trade : alk. paper)
ISBN 0-531-33243-8 (lib. bdg. : alk. paper)
[1. Brothers—Fiction. 2. Dinosaurs—Fiction.] I. Pearson, Tracey Campbell, ill.
II. Title. PZ7.D21955Gr   2000   [Fic]—dc21   99-30882

KEEP OUT!

Mark's Bed!

For Ricky and Steven,
good brothers, best friends
—T.D.

For Harry
—T.C.P.

big brother was big trouble for Gregory.
Mark slept in the best bed.
He rode up front in the car.
He filled the sofa, hogged the remote, and picked all the TV shows.

Gregory was smaller and second in line . . . and that *stunk*.

One afternoon Mom stepped out to run errands,
leaving Mark in charge as usual.

"You stinky stegosaurus!" hollered Gregory. "Get off my head!"
Gregory scrunched his eyes shut. The carpet felt scratchy,
and he didn't want to cry.

"Say you're sorry for hitting," Mark warned.

"Why should I?" whined Gregory.

Mark tightened his grip. "I'm twice your age and twice your size. *That's* why."

Mom got home in the nick of time. "Stop the fighting," she scolded.

"It's *his* fault," cried Gregory, wiping his nose. "He won't let me play basketball."

"The hoop is too high. He throws *wild*," Mark explained. "If I lift him up, he gets mad!"

Gregory rubbed his cheek. It was bumpy from the carpet, and there was fuzz in his nose. I'll score a basket *myself,* he thought. I'll score when I get *big.*

That night Mom served steak, Mark's favorite. Gregory pictured hooves on it. If only the meat would jump off his plate and run back to the butcher.

Mom bit into a piece. "Delicious," she said, smiling.

"Have some," said Dad. "Don't you want to get big like Mark?"

Gregory clenched his fork. He didn't want to get big like Mark. He wanted to get *bigger.*

Gregory began to chew. His small mouth tingled.

Ping Pong Pop!

His baby teeth bulged from his gums. The harder he chewed, the sharper they got.

Gregory picked up the rest of his steak. He shredded the meat easily. "Rum-scrum-num-scrum-yum." Then he lifted his dish, licked it clean, and gulped that down too.

"MORE MEAT!" howled Gregory, who grew bigger and taller while the table beneath him seemed shorter and smaller.

"How's this?" asked Mom in a tiny voice from below. She held up a bite on her fork.

"MORE!" he roared.

"But that's the end of the steak," said Dad.

"Okay," said Gregory. "No meat? No matter . . . I eat brother."

Mom and Dad tore through the freezer. Burgers and wieners soared through the air. Gregory chomped on the rock-solid meat, savoring each icy bite. Still, it wasn't enough.

"I am G-Rex!" stormed Gregory, pounding his chest. "Powerful, meat-eating dinosaur. Get more meat or I eat Mark!"

Dad grabbed the car keys, Mom snatched her purse, and they sped down the road to buy more.

"*Ooooo,*" crooned Gregory. "G-Rex see so *good.*"

The Pot Roast Palace sparkled in the distance. It filled the street with
the scent of simmering meat.

"Pot rooooooast dinnertime!" Gregory bellowed.

"You finished your dinner," Dad reminded him. "Two of them!"

"No meat? No matter," said Gregory, dreaming of a brother sandwich.
The rumble of his stomach made the little car lurch.

Gregory peered in the drive-thru window of the restaurant.
Pot roast drippings perfumed the air. "MEAT!" he roared at the
fast-food servers. "FEED G-REX *NOW*!"

They hurled bucket after bucket of meat his way. Then, one
by one, they fainted. His dinosaur teeth were terrifying . . .
but his breath was even scarier.

"GRAR! RAAR! RAARRR!"

Gregory ate in all the best places.

When he was full at last, the family headed for home.

"Tiny Mark sleep in tub," said Gregory, eyes twinkling.

"G-Rex get *two* beds."

"No fair!" cried Mark. "Sleep in your own!"

Gregory stayed up all night. He did not have to go to sleep . . .
not ever.

At breakfast Gregory wrestled Mark for a thin strip of bacon.
"MORE MEAT!" he roared. So they fed him.

"MORE FUN!" he sang. So they let him take shots at the hoop.

SWISH!

SLAM!

DUNK!

Gregory was still throwing wild.

As the week passed, Mom and Dad grew weary of his shouting. Mark got stiff from the tub. And all the restaurants ran out of meat. Careworn and cross, Gregory's family dropped in on Aunt Fanny next door.

"GRAR! RAAR! RAARRR!" Gregory roared through the empty rooms, but roaring alone was no fun. As the day dragged on, he could barely manage a grunt.

Gregory looked through the bedroom window. He watched Mark
bounce a ball to Aunt Fanny. **Thunk-thunk. Thunk-thunk.**
"Up for an Aunt-Fanny-dunk?" she asked.
Mark held her up to the metal rim, and she slam-dunked the
big orange ball. "You're almost as light as Gregory," he said.
"Whee!" squealed Aunt Fanny. "Do it again!"

Gregory's tail drooped. They were having
fun without him.
"No Mark to play with," Gregory wailed.
He slammed his fist and thumped his tail.
BUM BUM BUM.

The walls shook . . . the shelves trembled . . .
and **WHOOSH!** Mark's best basketball
trophy went crashing to the floor.

The plastic figure was in pieces. Gregory tried to fix it, but his dinosaur hands were too big for small things.

"Mark's best trophy," he said, shedding dinosaur tears.

One fat drop tumbled to his feet.

Pop Gnop Gnip!

Gregory's teeth prickled. His big body shriveled, and his long tail disappeared.

Small Gregory was back on the fuzzy carpet.

"You broke my very best one!" yelled Mark in his biggest voice of all.
"I didn't mean to!" cried Gregory. "Can we fix it?"
Mark studied the parts. "Can you hold them while I glue?"
Gregory nodded. His small hands could hold small things.

Thunk . . . thunk . . . thunk . . . The ball felt heavy in
Gregory's hands, and the hoop seemed higher than last time.

"Clutch the ball, bend your knees, and toss," said Mark.

Gregory tossed, again and again. Just when he thought he
could toss no more, **swish**. The basketball slid through the hoop.

"Score!" shouted Gregory. "Let's play more!"

Mark's eyes widened. "Up for a little-brother-dunk?"

"Way up!" said Gregory, racing for the ball.

Mark and Gregory played until dark.
A big brother could be *big* fun.